FIVE MINUTE
Traditional Tales

FIVE MINUTE
Traditional Tales

Written by
Derek Hall, Alison Morris
and Louisa Somerville

SIENA

Illustrated by
Anna Cattermole, Virginia Margerison, Paula Martyr,
Martin Orme, Sara Silcock, Gillian Toft, Jenny Williams

Designed by Louise Millar

This is a Siena Book
Siena is an imprint of Parragon

First published in Great Britain in 1998 by
PARRAGON, 13 Whiteladies Road,
Clifton, Bristol BS8 1PB

Created and produced for PARRAGON by
Linda Watters Book Packaging
8 Trent Close, Shenley
Herts WD7 9HX, UK

ISBN 0-75252-696-0

Printed in Singapore

Contents

Introduction

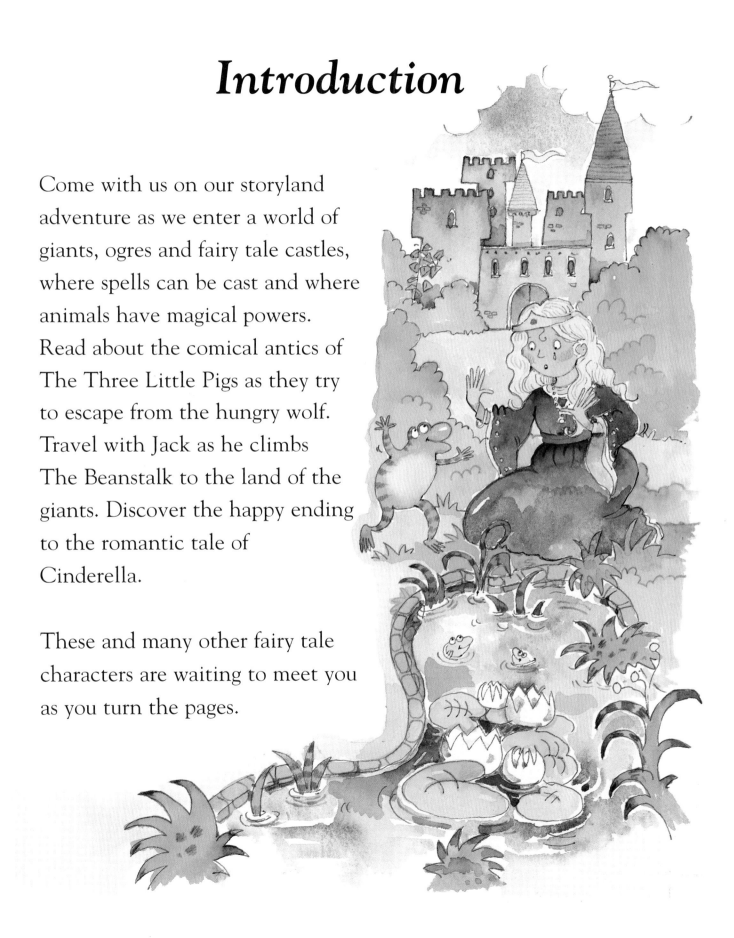

Come with us on our storyland
adventure as we enter a world of
giants, ogres and fairy tale castles,
where spells can be cast and where
animals have magical powers.
Read about the comical antics of
The Three Little Pigs as they try
to escape from the hungry wolf.
Travel with Jack as he climbs
The Beanstalk to the land of the
giants. Discover the happy ending
to the romantic tale of
Cinderella.

These and many other fairy tale
characters are waiting to meet you
as you turn the pages.

The Frog Prince

There was once a king who had but one daughter. Being his only child, she wanted for nothing. She had a nursery full of toys, a pony to ride and a wardrobe bursting with pretty dresses. But, for all this, the princess was lonely. "How I wish I had someone to play with," she sighed.

The princess's favourite toy was a beautiful golden ball. Every day she would play with her ball in the palace garden. When she threw the ball up in the air, it seemed to take off of its own accord and touch the clouds before landing in the princess's hands again.

One windy day the princess was playing in the garden as usual. She threw her golden ball high into the air, but instead of returning to her hands, the wind blew the ball into the fishpond. The princess ran to the pond, but to her dismay the ball had sunk right to the bottom. "Whatever shall I do?" wailed the girl. "Now I have lost my favourite toy." And she sat down beside the pond and cried.

All at once she heard a loud PLOP! and a large green frog landed on the grass beside her. "Eeeuugh! Go away you nasty thing!" screamed the princess.

To her astonishment, the frog spoke to her. "I heard you crying," he said in a gentle voice, "and I wondered what the matter was. Can I help you in any way?"

"Why, yes!" exclaimed the princess, once she had got over the shock of being addressed by a frog. "My ball has sunk to the bottom of the pond. Would you fish it out for me?"

"Of course I will," replied the frog. "But in return, what will you give me if I do?"

"You can have my jewels, my finest clothes and even my crown if you will find my ball," said the princess hastily, for she was truly eager to get her favourite toy back.

"I do not want your jewels, your clothes or your crown," replied the frog. "I would like to be your friend. I want to return with you to the palace and eat from your golden plate and sip from your golden cup. At night I want to sleep on a cushion made of silk next to your bed and I want you to kiss me goodnight before I go to sleep, too."

"I promise all you ask," said the girl, "if only you will find my golden ball."

"Remember what you have promised," said the frog, as he dived deep into the pond. At last he surfaced again with the ball and threw it on to the grass beside the princess. She was so overjoyed she forgot all about thanking the frog – let alone her promise – and ran all the way back to the palace.

That evening the king, the queen and the princess were having dinner in the great hall of the palace, when a courtier approached the king and said, "Your majesty, there is a frog at the door who says the princess has promised to share her dinner with him."

"Is this true?" demanded the king, turning to the princess and looking rather angry.

"Yes, it is," said the princess in a small voice. And she told her father the whole story.

"When a promise is made it must be kept, my girl," said the king. "You must ask the frog to dine with you."

Presently, the frog hopped into the great hall and round to where the princess was sitting. With a great leap he was up on the table beside her. She stifled a scream.

"You promised to let me eat from your golden plate," said the frog, tucking into the princess's food. The princess felt quite sick and pushed the plate away from her. Then to her horror the frog dipped his long tongue into her golden cup and drank every drop. "It's what you promised," he reminded her.

When he had finished, the frog stretched his long, green limbs, yawned and said, "Now I feel quite sleepy. Please take me to your room."

"Do I have to?" the princess pleaded with her father.

"Yes, you do," said the king sternly. "The frog helped you when you were in need and you made him a promise."

So the princess carried the frog to her bedroom but as they reached the door she said, "My bedroom's very warm. I'm sure you'd be more comfortable out here where it's cool."

But as she opened the bedroom door, the frog leaped from her hand and landed on her bed.

"You promised that I could sleep on a silk cushion next to your bed," said the frog.

"Yes, yes, of course," said the princess looking with horror at the froggy footprints on her clean, white sheets. She called to her maid to bring a cushion.

The frog jumped on to the cushion and looked as though he was going to sleep.

"Good," thought the princess, "he's forgotten about my final promise."

But just as she was about to get into bed, he opened his eyes and said, "What about my goodnight kiss?"

"Oh, woe is me," thought the princess as she closed her eyes and pursed her lips towards the frog's cold and clammy face and kissed him.

"Open your eyes," said a voice that didn't sound a bit like the frog's. She opened her eyes and there, standing before her, was a prince. The princess stood there in dumbstruck amazement.

"Thank you," said the prince. "You have broken a spell cast upon me by a wicked witch. She turned me into a frog and said the spell would only be broken if a princess would eat with me, sleep beside me and kiss me."

They ran to tell the king what had happened. He was delighted and said, "You may live in the palace from now on, for my daughter needs a friend." And indeed, the prince and princess became the best of friends and she was never lonely again. He taught her to play football with the golden ball and she taught him to ride her pony. One day, many years later, they were married and had lots of children. And, do you know, their children were particularly good at leapfrog.

Jack and the Beanstalk

Once there was an old woman who lived with her only son Jack in a tumble-down cottage in a meadow by a pine forest. The old woman and her son were very poor, and they were getting poorer as each winter passed. After one particularly cruel and cold winter, when the ground had frozen like ice, the old woman turned to her son and said, "Jack, there is only one thing left to sell. You must take the old brown cow to market tomorrow and sell her for her meat – she is all that is left between us and starvation, so mind you get a good price!"

So the next morning Jack took the old brown cow and started the long journey into town.

Halfway through his journey, Jack stopped to eat his crust of bread. Just then a farmer passed by, and stopped to chat. After Jack told the farmer where he was heading and why, the farmer looked at the old cow and scratched his chin thoughtfully. He put his hand into his pocket and said to Jack, "I'll swap you these dried beans for your old brown cow."

Jack looked at the beans in the farmer's hand and shook his head. "I'm sorry," he said, "but I must take the old brown cow to sell at the market so that my mother and I can buy bread."

The farmer promised Jack that if he would swap the cow for the beans, Jack would make his fortune. Jack finally agreed, and went home with the beans in his pocket.

When he got home he told his mother about his adventure, but his mother cried when Jack told her the old brown cow was gone and all they had were dried beans. She snatched the beans from Jack's hand and threw them out of the window in anger.

17

Just as dawn was breaking, Jack woke up to discover a huge beanstalk had shot up during the night right outside his window. He ran downstairs and looked at the huge beanstalk – it was taller than even the tallest trees in the nearby pine forest, and disappeared into the clouds. Jack decided to climb the beanstalk.

Jack climbed and climbed. He climbed so high that when he looked down, the tumble-down cottage was a tiny speck far below. The top of the beanstalk was still out of sight so he climbed some more. Eventually, Jack climbed through the clouds and was amazed when he got to the top of the stalk to discover another land very different from the one he'd left below.

Everything was HUGE. The trees were enormous, the grass came up to Jack's shoulder, and in the distance was the largest castle he had ever seen. Just as Jack was starting out towards the castle, he heard a thunderous rustling in the grass behind him, and he looked round to see a huge giantess towering above him.

"Mmmmm – not much meat on those bones," she said, "so I won't bother to eat you. However, you might come in handy around the house to do all the boring old chores." And with that she picked Jack up and popped him into the pocket of her apron, and carried him into the castle. On the way, she warned Jack not to let her husband, the giant, see him. "The last house boy I had was made into jam, and he's looking for another to pound into bread," she said quite calmly.

Soon Jack felt the castle shudder at the approach of the giant, and he hid behind the coal scuttle. "Fee Fi Fo Fum," roared the giant. "I smell the blood of an Englishman. Be him live or be him dead, I'll break his bones to make my bread."

"Don't be silly," said the giantess, "you've never once changed your socks, and it's your feet you can smell."

Satisfied with this answer, the giant sat down and started to count his money. Jack sneaked a peek from his hiding place and saw a mountain of gold coins piled high on the table. Then the giant scooped it all back into the purse, put his feet on the table, and fell sound asleep.

19

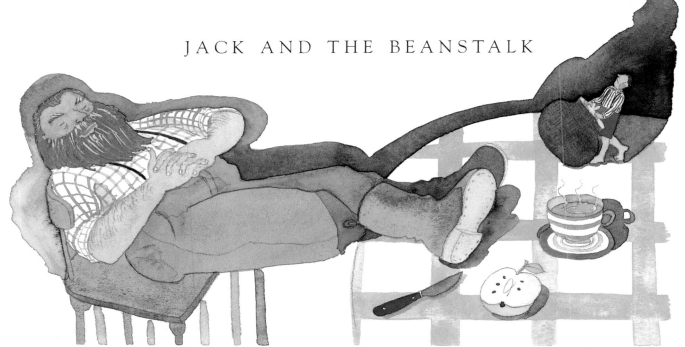

When the thunderous snores convinced Jack that it was safe, he sneaked up on to the table. The purse was within reach, and Jack dragged it to the edge of the table where it fell with a tremendous KLUNK on to the floor. The giant slept on. Quickly Jack climbed down and dragged the purse to the castle door, and down to the meadow, and then down, down, down the beanstalk.

When Jack finally got back with his treasure he showed it to his mother who hugged him with joy, and warned him never to climb the beanstalk again.

But Jack decided that he would go back to the castle to find some more treasures, and when morning came again he got dressed and went down to the beanstalk to start the long climb all over again. Before he left the house, he tied a red scarf around his head, and painted freckles on his face, so that when he reached the top of the beanstalk and once again met the giantess, she would not recognise him.

20

Once again, she picked Jack up and popped him into her apron pocket, and warned him about the terrible giant. Once more, Jack hid as the castle trembled at the giant's approach.

"Fee Fi Fo Fum," roared the giant, "I smell the blood of an Englishman. Be him live or be him dead, I'll break his bones to make my bread."

"Tsk tsk," said the giantess, "the only thing you can smell is your armpits which have never been washed."

Satisfied with this answer, the giant sat down and called for his hen to be brought to him. Jack peeked around and saw to his amazement that the hen had laid a beautiful golden egg! Before long, the giant rested his head once more, then fell fast asleep.

When Jack heard the snoring, he sneaked up on to the table and gently took the hen, then quickly climbed down and carried it to the castle door, and down to the meadow and then down, down, down the beanstalk. When Jack returned once more with his treasure, his mother was waiting for him, and when Jack showed her the hen, she hugged him and begged him never to climb the beanstalk again.

But once again, Jack thought about the treasures in the castle, and the following morning he went down to the beanstalk to start the long climb all over again.

21

This time before he left the house, he tied a blue scarf around his head, and rubbed dirt into his face, and once again when he reached the top of the beanstalk and met the giantess, she did not recognise him. As before, she picked Jack up and popped him into her apron pocket, and warned him about the giant.

Again, the castle trembled at the approach of the giant. "Fee Fi Fo Fum. I smell the blood of an Englishman. Be him live or be him dead, I'll break his bones to make my bread," said the giant once again.

"What rot!" said the giantess. "That'll be all those bugs in your hair that's never been combed!"

Once more satisfied, the giant sat down and called for his harp to be brought to him. When the giant plucked at the strings of the harp, it magically started to sing in a clear soprano voice! The giant was soon lulled into a deep slumber across the table, and Jack wanted the beautiful harp so much that he didn't even wait for the snores! Jack climbed up to the table and put his hands on the harp to sneak it from under the nose of the sleeping giant, but to his horror, the harp started to shriek, "Help! Help! I'm being stolen."

22

The giant woke up. With a mighty roar he shouted, "Fee Fi Fo Fum, I smell the blood of an Englishman. Be him live or be him dead, I'll break his bones to make my bread." And with that he raced after Jack. But the giant wasn't as nimble as Jack, and Jack was able to rush out of the castle, down to the meadow and reach the top of the beanstalk with the giant in pursuit. Jack climbed down as quickly as possible, but the giant was not far behind him. The further down Jack climbed, the closer the giant got to him. When Jack was nearly at the bottom, he called to his mother to fetch the wood axe, and then Jack jumped the rest of the way to the ground. He grabbed at the axe and started to chop furiously at the stalk. The giant was almost down when the beanstalk crashed to the ground – right on top of him! The giant was squashed to nothing.

Now, with all the gold they had, Jack and his mother never needed to worry about money again.

Little Red Riding Hood

There was once a little girl who was given a lovely, bright red cloak by her grandmother. The little girl loved this cloak very much. She loved it so much in fact that she never wanted to take it off, and was always wearing it. Because of this, she became known as Little Red Riding Hood.

One sunny morning, Little Red Riding Hood's mother asked her if she would take some cakes and apple juice to her grandmother, who was ill.

Little Red Riding Hood loved her grandmother very much, and was pleased to be going to visit her.

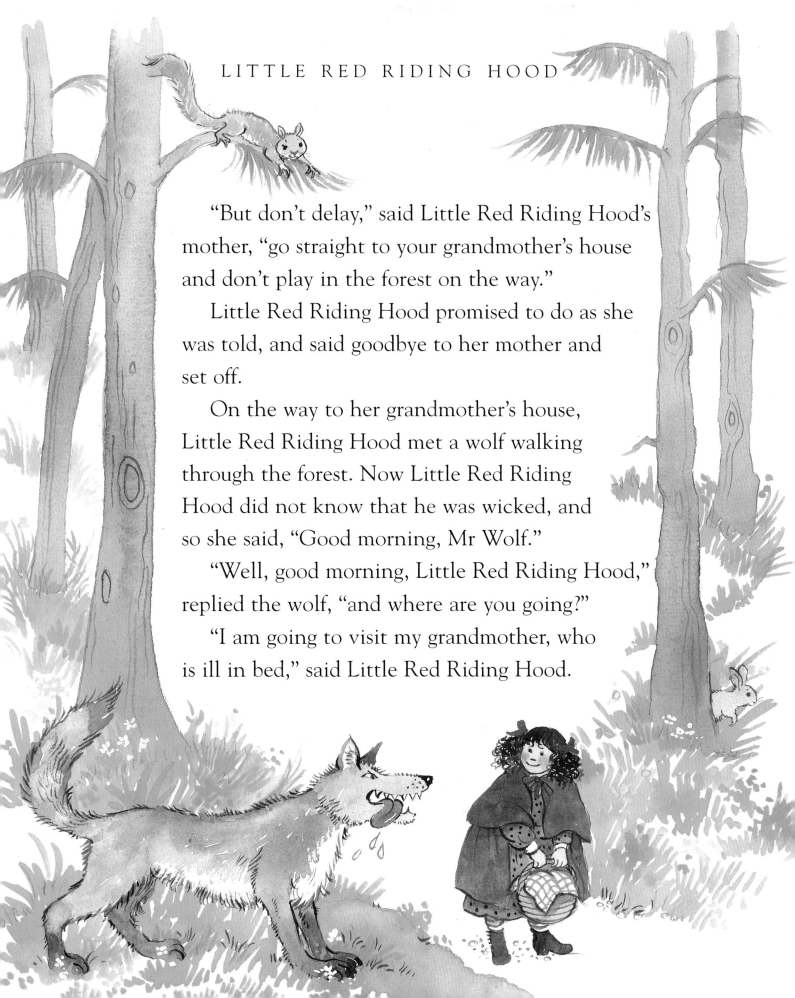

"But don't delay," said Little Red Riding Hood's mother, "go straight to your grandmother's house and don't play in the forest on the way."

Little Red Riding Hood promised to do as she was told, and said goodbye to her mother and set off.

On the way to her grandmother's house, Little Red Riding Hood met a wolf walking through the forest. Now Little Red Riding Hood did not know that he was wicked, and so she said, "Good morning, Mr Wolf."

"Well, good morning, Little Red Riding Hood," replied the wolf, "and where are you going?"

"I am going to visit my grandmother, who is ill in bed," said Little Red Riding Hood.

"What have you got in your basket, Little Red Riding Hood?" asked the wolf.

"I've got some cakes and a jug of apple juice," said Little Red Riding Hood.

"And where does your grandmother live?" asked the wolf.

"She lives in the forest, not far from here," said Little Red Riding Hood. "Her house is easy to find. It's right next to the lake."

Now the reason that the wolf was asking all these questions was because he really wanted to gobble up Little Red Riding Hood and her grandmother. Suddenly he thought of a cunning plan. "Little Red Riding Hood," he said, "I have an idea! Why don't you pick some of those beautiful flowers which are growing in the forest and give them to your sick grandmother?"

"What a good idea," said Little Red Riding Hood. "My grandmother would be so pleased to have some of these pretty flowers. I'm sure they would make her feel better."

And with that, she set about picking a big bunch of the prettiest flowers she could find. In fact, she was so busy looking for flowers that she didn't see the crafty wolf skip away and make off towards her grandmother's house. The wolf soon came to the house, and knocked on the door.

"Who is it?" said Grandmother.

"It's me, Little Red Riding Hood," said the wolf. "I've brought you some cakes and a jug of apple juice."

"Come in, come in, my dear," said Grandmother, "the door isn't locked."

The wolf then went into the house, and as soon as he saw the old lady lying in bed, he ran straight over to her and gobbled her up. Next he put on her nightdress and her frilly night cap and jumped into her bed, pulling the bed clothes up to his chin.

In a little while, Little Red Riding Hood – who had by now picked a lovely bunch of flowers for her grandmother – came hurrying up the garden path. The door to her grandmother's house was still open and so she went inside and walked over to the bed. Little Red Riding Hood could only see a little bit of her face poking out from the bed clothes.

"My, Grandmother, what big ears you have," said Little Red Riding Hood.

28

"All the better to hear you with, my dear," said the wolf.

"My, Grandmother, what big eyes you have," said Little Red Riding Hood.

"All the better to see you with, my dear," said the wolf.

"My, Grandmother, what big hands you have," said Little Red Riding Hood.

"All the better to hold you tight with, my dear," said the wolf.

"My, Grandmother, what big teeth you have," said Little Red Riding Hood.

"All the better to eat you with, my dear," cried the wolf. And with that he jumped out of bed and gobbled her up.

The wolf felt very full and rather sleepy after he had eaten Little Red Riding Hood. After all, he'd already just eaten her grandmother, too. So he went back to bed and fell asleep, snoring loudly.

Just then, a hunter was passing the house and heard the snoring. He looked through the window, and when he saw the wolf lying in bed, he realised that the wolf must have eaten the old lady. So, while the wolf was still sleeping, the hunter took his knife and cut open the wolf's stomach. To the hunter's great surprise, out popped Little Red Riding Hood and her grandmother. Luckily, the hunter had arrived just in time and both were still alive.

Little Red Riding Hood and her grandmother both thanked the hunter for saving them, and the hunter took the dead wolf's skin and went home.

Little Red Riding Hood's grandmother ate the cakes and drank the apple juice, and soon she was feeling much better. And Little Red Riding Hood? Well, she decided that she would never talk to a wolf again!

The Sleeping Beauty

A long time ago, in a land far away, there ruled the happiest king and queen who had ever lived. They were especially happy because after years of hoping in vain, they had finally been blessed by the birth of a beautiful baby daughter.

The king and queen were so happy that they decided to celebrate by throwing a huge banquet for their family and friends, and all the most important people in the kingdom. As they sat down to write the invitations, a worried look crossed the queen's face. "The Countess Griselda will be very angry if she doesn't get an invitation," she said to her husband.

The king's face went very pale for a moment. Then he shook his head and said, "No, she must not be invited. Griselda is wicked and mean. I do not wish her to cast her eyes on our beautiful daughter." With that they continued writing the invitations.

The day of the banquet arrived, and all the most important people took their places in the Great Hall. Before the celebrations began, a line formed to pay homage to the little Princess Angelina, who lay sleeping in her cradle next to the king and queen's thrones. Twelve people stood in line, and one by one they stepped forward to give their gift to the sleeping princess.

First up stepped the good Lady Soprano, who touched the baby's throat with her forefinger and declared that the princess would have a voice like an angel. Next came the Archduke Ernest, and with a light touch on her forehead he vowed she would grow to be very wise. Next came the Duchess Rose, who stroked the baby's face and declared she would blossom into the most beautiful flower in the kingdom.

One by one the guests came forward and bestowed the gifts of patience, kindness, faith, grace, fortune, virtue, happiness and sweetness. With just one guest left to give her gift, there was a terrible noise outside the Great Hall and the huge doors were thrown open in a rage. In stormed the Countess Griselda. The Great Hall fell silent as she slowly approached the sleeping baby. The king and queen jumped to their feet to protect their little one, but Griselda swept them both aside.

As they looked up in fear at Griselda, she turned to them and whispered in a hard, cruel voice, "I think you mislaid my invitation, but I have come to give my gift to the precious child anyway." As she bent over the child she cackled, "To this child I bestow the gift of absolute health until the day she dies." As relief showed itself on the faces of the crowd, she roared with laughter and bellowed, "Which is why it is such a pity she will not live beyond her sixteenth birthday!" The crowd was stunned as she continued, "A spindle shall be her end. A common peasant's spindle." And she touched the tip of the middle finger on the baby's right hand. She then clapped her hands together and a great roll of thunder was heard, before a terrible wind swept through the open doors blowing out all the candles. When the doors were shut and the candles re-lit, Griselda had disappeared, leaving only her terrible spell behind her.

As the king and queen wept, they did not see the final guest who had yet to bestow her gift. The Marquess Maria bent over Angelina and whispered, "I cannot take away the evil of Griselda, but I can give you the greatest gift of all. I give you the gift of love. On that terrible day to come you shall not die a death, but sleep, little one, sleep deep and peacefully as you sleep now, until love comes to rescue you." She placed her forefinger on the baby's heart and then was gone.

The king and queen were in despair, and they demanded that every spindle in the kingdom be destroyed. But they couldn't sleep a single night without worrying, and a day didn't pass that they let the little princess out of their sight for a moment.

Angelina grew, and with every passing year she became sweeter, and with every passing day she became more beautiful.

The day before Angelina's sixteenth birthday arrived and as the king looked at his daughter he felt a pang of sorrow, for he knew that he could not stop her destiny.

Her birthday arrived, and for the first time ever the king and queen allowed her to roam freely around the castle. The king had ordered a huge celebration to be prepared in the Great Hall for later in the day, and Angelina had tremendous fun watching the cooks prepare delicious pies, pastries and cakes in the kitchens. She watched the servants making garlands of flowers and roamed through all the corridors to watch the preparations.

In a corridor off the Great Hall, she followed a trail of petals, winding first one way and then another, up and up into a turret in the castle that she had never visited before. When she reached the top, a door swung open and in the corner of the darkened room a little old lady sat spinning some yarn.

"Come closer, my child," she beckoned.

Angelina moved closer.

"Closer still," she urged.

When Angelina was close enough the old woman

36

reached out to Angelina's right hand and pulled it to the spindle needle. The princess gave a gasp of pain as it pricked her middle finger, and then she fell into the deepest, most peaceful of sleeps. And as she fell asleep, the whole castle fell asleep, too. The cooks fell asleep at the roasting spit. The horses fell asleep in the stable. The king fell asleep on his throne. Everything in the castle came to a complete and utter standstill.

The years passed by, and with every passing year the thorns that grew around the castle became thicker and higher, and the legend of the sleeping beauty spread to distant lands. As time went on, many brave princes tried to cut down the thorns, but not one succeeded and countless young men were lost forever in the forest of thorns.

Many years had passed before one brave prince awoke from a dream in which the angelic voice of a strange girl had called to him from a thorn bush. He asked his father the meaning of the dream, but the king shook his head and said it was best he didn't know.

But the following night, the young prince once again dreamed of the strange girl, and this time he saw the princess deep in sleep but calling to be freed. The prince was enchanted. She was the most beautiful girl he had ever seen, and again he asked his father who she was. Again the king refused to say anything, but when the prince's dreams continued and the prince felt he would rather die than live without the princess, the king relented, and told his son of the sleeping princess far, far away.

The prince lost no time, and set off on a voyage that lasted a year and a day. Along the way he heard tales of the princes who had tried before him and the fate they had met; some had been turned to stone, some had turned to water, and others had simply vanished without trace, but none had succeeded.

The prince finally reached his destination and stood outside the walls of the thorn forest. He knelt and said a prayer for all the lost souls who had tried before him, and then he raised his sword to strike the thorns. In that instant, a vision of the princess rose up to him, and he was so overcome with love that he dropped his sword and tried to touch the vision. As he reached out he touched the thorns, and as he touched the thorns, they turned into flowers in his hands. The further into the forest he went, the more the forest bowed down before him, until all that separated him from the princess was a carpet of roses. The prince raced past the sleeping horses, cooks and the king and ran up the stairs to where the princess lay. He bent over her sleeping form and placed a single kiss upon her rosy lips. In that instant, she opened her eyes – love had set her free.

The cooks yawned at their spit and woke up. The horses neighed their yawns and woke up. The king yawned on his throne and woke up. Everyone in the castle woke up. When the prince led the princess to her father he cried with joy, and granted him any wish that he could choose. The prince asked for the princess's hand in marriage, and they both lived happily ever after.

Goldilocks and the Three Bears

There once lived a little girl who had long, golden hair. Because of this, everyone knew her as Goldilocks. Goldilocks and her mother lived together in a cosy little cottage in the forest.

"Would you like some pretty flowers?" Goldilocks asked her mother one day. "I will pick you some if you like."

"That would be lovely, my dear," said her mother. "But mind you don't get lost. Don't stray too far, and don't be too long."

Goldilocks gave her mother a big hug and promised to be careful. She picked up her little flower basket and skipped off into the forest to look for flowers.

First she came upon some big, bright daffodils. She picked a few and placed them in her basket. A little further on, she spied some pretty bluebells and so she picked a bunch of those as well. Then she saw, even further on, some lovely marigolds which she also picked and put into her basket.

Well, Goldilocks was so busy picking all these wonderful flowers that she wandered further and further into the forest. Suddenly she realised that she was lost. She didn't know which way to turn. She was also beginning to feel very hungry and tired.

Just when she was wondering what to do next, she saw a small cottage nestling among the trees. She went up to it and looked through the windows, but couldn't see anyone inside. But the door was open and so she went in. Inside the cottage she found a table laid out with three bowls of steaming porridge. There was a big bowl, a medium-sized bowl and a little bowl. The table also had three chairs arranged around it, one next to each of the bowls of porridge. There was a big chair, a medium-sized chair and a little chair.

Goldilocks was so tired that she simply had to sit down. First she sat down in the big chair, but it was very hard and lumpy. It wasn't comfortable at all. Then she tried the medium-sized chair, but that didn't feel comfortable either. At last, she tried the little chair, but as soon as she sat down in it – it broke! She was too heavy for the little chair. "Oh dear," thought Goldilocks.

Instead of sitting down, she thought she would have some porridge as she was still very hungry. First she took a spoonful of porridge from the big bowl. But it was too hot, and so she couldn't eat it. Then she tried a spoonful from the medium-sized bowl, but it was too lumpy. So she tried a spoonful from the little bowl. And guess what? It tasted so delicious that she ate it all up!

"Oh, I do feel sleepy," yawned Goldilocks after she had finished the porridge in the little bowl. "I wonder if there is a nice, comfortable bed I can sleep in."

So she went upstairs and found a bedroom with three beds in it. There was a big bed, a medium-sized bed and a little bed. First she tried the big bed, but it was very hard and didn't feel comfortable at all. Next she tried the medium-sized bed, but it was too soft and that didn't feel comfortable either. Finally, she tried the little bed. It was just right – warm and cosy. Soon she was fast asleep.

Just then, the family of three bears who lived in the cottage came back from their walk in the forest. As soon as they came in through the front door, they knew someone had been there.

"Who has been sitting in my chair?" said Daddy Bear, in a deep, gruff voice.

"And who has been sitting in my chair?" asked Mummy Bear in a softer voice.

"Who has broken my chair?" cried Baby Bear in a squeaky voice.

Then the three bears looked on the table.

"Someone has been trying my porridge," said Daddy Bear.

"And someone has been trying my porridge, too," said Mummy Bear.

"Who has eaten all my porridge?" said Baby Bear, who by now was very upset and sobbing big tears.

Upstairs went the three bears and into their bedroom.

"Who has been sleeping in my bed?" asked Daddy Bear.

"And who has been sleeping in my bed?" asked Mummy Bear.

Suddenly, Baby Bear gave a cry of surprise. "Look!" he yelled.

"There's someone sleeping in my bed."

46

Goldilocks woke up with a start when she heard all the noise. She looked up to see the three bears staring down at her. She was so frightened that she jumped straight out of bed, down the stairs and out through the front door. Then she ran and ran until she arrived back home to her own cottage again.

And do you know, that was the last that the three bears ever saw of Goldilocks!

The Three Little Pigs

Once upon a time there were three little pigs who lived on a farm with their mother and father. They decided that, although they were just little pigs, they were quite grown up enough to make their way in the big wide world, so one day they set off together to make their fortunes.

After they had walked for quite some time, one of the little pigs started to feel rather tired. Just then, a farmer went by on his haycart.

"Hey, stop cart," the first little pig yelled. "You stronger brothers go on without me," he said. "This hay is light enough and soft enough for my house." And with that his brothers left the little pig with his pile of hay, and carried on their journey.

A little further down the road, the second little pig grew very tired. Just then, they passed by a forester cutting wood.

"Would you sell me some of your wood?" asked the second little pig. "This wood isn't too heavy and it isn't too rough for my house – it's just right." And with that the third little pig carried on his journey. Soon, even the third little pig grew very tired, and up ahead he spotted a builder making a wall out of stone.

"Aha," he thought, "that's exactly what I need to build my house, as it's strong and tough, just like me." And so he bought some stone and built himself a house.

That evening, just as the first little pig was settling comfortably in his bed of hay, he heard a rustling outside the house. He easily parted the hay with his hands to look outside, and gulped in fright when he saw the big bad wolf looking at him greedily.

"Little piggy, little piggy, will you let me in?"

"Not on the hairs of my chinny chin chin, I will not let you in," shuddered the first little pig.

"Then I'll huff, and I'll puff, and I'll blow your house down," said the big bad wolf.

And sure enough, he gave a little huff, and he gave a little puff, and with very little effort he blew the house down. Before the straw had settled to the ground, the little pig ran away as fast as his little legs would carry him to the home of his nearest brother.

The next evening, just as the two brothers were sitting down at their wooden table to eat their dinner, they heard scratching and sniffing outside the house. They peeked through the wooden window and gasped in alarm when they saw the big bad wolf staring at them hungrily. His stomach rumbled loudly.

"Little piggies, little piggies, will you let me in?"

"Not on the hairs of our chinny chin chins, we will not let you in," trembled the little pigs.

"Then I'll huff, and I'll puff, and I'll blow your house down," said the big bad wolf.

And sure enough, he huffed a bit, and he puffed a bit, and with a bit of effort he blew the house down. Before the planks of wood had crashed to the ground, the two pigs ran away as fast as their little legs would carry them to the home of their brother.

The next evening, just as the three brothers were making the fire to warm their toes, they heard crunching and crashing outside the house. The third little pig pulled a tiny stone out of the wall to make a peephole, and they all shrieked in terror when they saw the big bad wolf staring at them ravenously. His stomach grumbled even louder, and he was smacking his lips with glee at the feast waiting just a short breath away!

"Little piggies, little piggies, will you let me in?"

"Not on the hairs of our chinny chin chins, we will not let you in," quaked the three little pigs.

"Then I'll huff, and I'll puff, and I'll blow your house down," said the big bad wolf.

And sure enough, he took a big huff, and he took a big puff, and with a big effort he blew. But the house didn't blow down. So he took a bigger huff, and he took a bigger puff, and with the biggest of efforts he blew. But the house still didn't blow down. So he filled his lungs as full as he could and with a mighty effort he blew and blew and blew! And the house stayed up!

With that the big bad wolf started to climb up the stone wall to the chimney on the roof. The three little pigs looked around the stark stone room and then at each other in dismay – there was nowhere in here to hide, and nowhere left to run. They would have to stand and fight the big bad wolf!

Suddenly one of the little pigs had an idea, and whispered it into the ears of his brothers. They all ran over to the fireplace and hooked a huge pot of water over the roaring fire. They heard the wolf climb into the chimney. The water in the pot started to steam. They heard the wolf climbing down the chimney. The water started to bubble. They heard the wolf slide the rest of the way down the chimney and he landed splash in the middle of the pot of now boiling water. PLOP!

"AAARRRRHHHHH!" screamed the big bad wolf, leaping immediately out of the boiling pot. The three little pigs ran around the room trying to get away from the wolf, as the big bad wolf ran around the room trying to cool down, until eventually he ran straight through the stone wall, leaving a huge big bad wolf shaped hole, and carried on running and screaming and shouting all the way through the woods. That was the last they ever saw of the big bad wolf.

The three little pigs knew they had beaten the wolf, and he would never trouble them again, so they decided to build a brand new, comfortable house to live in. They built the walls of tough, strong stone. They made tables of smooth, warm wood, and they gathered lots of sweet-smelling, soft fresh hay to make comfortable beds. It was the best house in the world, and they all lived in it happily ever after.

Cinderella

Once upon a time there was a beautiful young girl who lived with her widowed father. He had brought her up to be kind and gentle. All went well until the day the girl's father married again. His second wife was very proud of her house. Everything always had to be spotlessly clean. Worse than that, she had two spiteful daughters. All three had terrible tempers, and they hated the beautiful young girl with a vengeance. All day long from dawn to dusk she was made to scrub and clean, mend clothes and serve at the table. At night, while the household slept, there was coal to fetch, fires to be laid and the table to be set for breakfast the following day.

The stepmother gave her own two daughters the finest rooms in the house. To her stepdaughter, she gave the coldest attic room, with the hardest bed and a quilt cover that was so thin it barely kept out the winter chill. To keep warm, the poor girl had to sit in the chimney nook of the kitchen with her feet near the cinders. Because of this, her stepsisters nicknamed her Cinderella.

One day a footman called at the house to deliver an invitation. Cinderella carried it into the dining room where her stepsisters were having breakfast. "What have you there?" shrieked one of them, snatching the envelope from her hand. She tore it open with her long, polished nails. "Ooh!" she cried. "It's an invitation from the prince to attend a ball tomorrow night!"

The other sister jumped up and down with delight. "We're going to a ball!" she yelled.

"Am I invited, too?" asked Cinderella shyly.

"You?" cried the elder sister.

"You – invited to the palace ball?" cried the other sister, and they both burst into fits of laughter. The elder sister, who was very plump, laughed so much that she became quite breathless and had to ask Cinderella to loosen her corset.

The sisters spent the next day preparing for the ball. Cinderella was kept very busy, pressing and starching the girls' ballgowns, curling their hair and fixing bows and ribbons. They told her to lace their corsets extra tight to make them look slimmer. She was made to run hither and thither all day. "Fetch my pearl necklace!" called one.

"Polish my party shoes!" demanded the other. At last both sisters were ready to go, and set off by carriage to the ball. "Don't wait up!" they shouted out of the window to Cinderella, as the coach sped away.

Cinderella went back into the kitchen. Now the house seemed calm and quiet at last. She picked up a broom and danced slowly round the room, imagining that she was at the ball. "How wonderful it would be to go to the ball," she sighed wistfully, and sat down by the fire where it was warm and started to cry.

"Don't cry, my child," said a gentle voice.

Cinderella looked up to see a beautiful stranger standing before her. "Who are you?" said Cinderella.

"I am your fairy godmother," came the reply. "Now, dry your tears. Would you like to go to the ball?" said the fairy.

"Oh, yes please," cried Cinderella, leaping up.

"Then you shall go," said the fairy. "But first, run into the garden, and fetch me a nice fat pumpkin." Cinderella did as she was told. When she returned, the fairy godmother tapped the pumpkin with her magic wand and instantly it was transformed into a sparkling glass coach.

"Now we need some horses," said the fairy. At that moment there was a scuttling noise in the corner of the kitchen and four white mice popped out of a hole. In an instant the fairy godmother tapped them with her wand and they became four handsome white horses. "Now what about a footman," she said. Before Cinderella could speak she tapped Cinderella's black cat and there before her very eyes stood a footman. "Now there's just one more thing we need before you go," said the fairy, "and that's a coachman."

Cinderella looked about the kitchen and scratched her head.

Then she ran into the garden and came back with a live frog. "Will he do?" she asked her fairy godmother.

"Indeed he will," replied the fairy, tapping the frog. And suddenly there was a coachman standing by the coach.

"All aboard!" he cried.

Cinderella was just about to leap inside when her godmother called her back. "I nearly forgot something," she said.

The tip of her wand touched Cinderella's ragged clothes and Cinderella looked down to see, to her astonishment, that she was wearing the most beautiful ballgown that there ever was. At her neck glittered a diamond necklace and on her feet were a dainty pair of glass slippers. "Have a lovely time at the ball," said her godmother. "But do not stay a minute longer than midnight, for on the stroke of twelve, everything will be as it was before."

And with that, she vanished.

When Cinderella arrived at the ball, she found herself in a dazzling ballroom filled with people. Everyone stopped to stare at this beautiful girl, and soon the prince himself approached and asked her to dance. "Who is she?" people were asking. The prince and Cinderella danced together all evening. Her stepsisters watched, never once guessing who she was.

"Isn't she beautiful," remarked the elder sister jealously.

"Such a tiny waist – she might snap in two!" whispered the other spitefully, and they both roared with laughter.

When the banquet was served the prince insisted that Cinderella sit next to him, and after dinner they danced again. Cinderella was enjoying herself so much she forgot all about the time. It was only when the clock struck midnight that she remembered her godmother's warning. She fled from the ballroom without a backward glance. The prince hurried after her but she ran faster than he. As she sped down the steps her ballgown turned to rags and she dropped one of her glass slippers. The prince picked it up. By the time she reached home, Cinderella was exhausted.

61

Soon her sisters arrived home. "There was the most beautiful princess at the ball," said one.

"The prince fell in love with her, and he was deeply saddened when she left at midnight," said the other.

As for the prince, he spent all night with the glass slipper pressed to his cheek, mourning the loss of the most wonderful girl he had ever set eyes upon. The next morning he was determined to find her. He sent his servant to all corners of the kingdom. "I will marry the girl whose foot fits the slipper," he declared. Well, every princess, duchess and lady in the land tried on the slipper, but none of them could fit the tiny shoe on her foot.

At last the servant called at the house of Cinderella and her stepsisters. "Me first!" they cried, pushing each other out of the way. One sister tried on the slipper but her toes were so fat that she couldn't squeeze them into the dainty shoe. Then the other sister tried, but her toes were so long they wouldn't fit either.

Cinderella had been watching from her corner by the fire. Now she came forward. "May I try on the shoe?" she asked timidly.

The stepsisters shrieked, "Don't be absurd! You weren't even at the ball."

But the prince's servant said, "If you wish to try on the slipper, then you shall." Cinderella slid her foot into the glass slipper and of course it fitted perfectly. The stepsisters were completely speechless with rage.

At that moment there was a flash of bright light and Cinderella's fairy godmother appeared. She touched Cinderella with her magic wand and immediately the girl's rags were transformed into the ballgown that she had worn the night before. Then her sisters recognised the beautiful princess they had seen at the ball. They fell upon their knees and begged forgiveness for the way they had treated her, hoping that they, too, might be invited to the palace. The servant escorted Cinderella to the palace and when the prince saw her, he immediately asked her to marry him. At the wedding there was much rejoicing and the sisters were so well behaved that they, too, received marriage proposals and they all lived happily ever after.

63

The Ugly Duckling

Once upon a time, there was a mother duck who laid a clutch of six beautiful little eggs. One day, she looked into her nest in amazement. For there were her six small eggs but lying next to them was another egg that was much, much bigger than the others. "That's odd," she thought, and went back to sitting on the nest.

Soon, one by one, the smaller eggs hatched, and out came six pretty yellow ducklings. Yet the bigger egg still had not hatched.

The mother duck sat on the large egg for another day and another night until eventually the egg cracked, and out tumbled a seventh duckling.

But this one was very different. He was big, with scruffy grey feathers and large brown feet.

"You do look different from my other chicks," exclaimed the mother duck, "but never mind, I'm sure you've got a heart of gold." And she cuddled him to her with all the other ducklings. Sure enough, he was very sweet-natured and happily played alongside the other ducklings.

One day, the mother duck led her ducklings down to the river to learn to swim. One by one they jumped into the water and splashed about. But when the big grey duckling leaped into the water he swam beautifully. He could swim faster and further than any of his brothers or sisters. The other ducklings were jealous and began to resent him.

"You're a big ugly duckling," they hissed at him. "You don't belong here." And when their mother wasn't looking they chased him right away.

The ugly duckling felt very sad as he waddled away across the fields. "I know I'm not fluffy and golden like my brothers and sisters," he said to himself. "I may have scruffy grey feathers and big brown feet, but I'm just as good as they are – and I'm

66

better at swimming!" He sat down under a bush and started to cry. Just then he heard a terrible sound – CRACK! CRACK! It was the sound of a gun. There were men out there shooting ducks. Then, only a short way from where he was hiding, a dog rushed past him, sniffing the ground. The ugly duckling did not dare to move. He stayed under the bush until it was dark and only then did he feel it was safe to come out.

He set off, not knowing which way he was going until eventually, through the darkness, he saw a light shining. The light came from a cosy-looking cottage. The ugly duckling looked inside cautiously. He could see a fire burning in the hearth and sitting by the fire was an old woman with a hen and a cat.

"Come in, little duckling," said the old woman. "You are welcome to stay here. For now I can have duck's eggs each day as well as hen's eggs."

The ugly duckling was glad to warm himself by the fire. When the old lady had gone to bed, the hen and the cat cornered the duckling.

"Can you lay eggs?" enquired the hen.

"No," replied the duckling.

"Can you catch mice?" demanded the cat.

"No," replied the miserable duckling.

"Well, you're no use then, are you?" they sneered.

The next day, the old woman scolded the duckling: "You've been here a whole day and not one egg! You're no use, are you?"

So the ugly duckling waddled off out of the cottage. "I know when I'm not wanted," he said to himself mournfully.

He wandered along for a very long time until at last he reached a lake where he could live without anyone to bother him. He lived on the lake for many months. Gradually the days got shorter and the nights longer. The wind blew the leaves off the trees. Winter came and the weather turned bitterly cold. The lake froze over and the ugly duckling shivered under the reeds at the lake's edge. He was desperately cold, hungry and lonely, but he had nowhere else to go.

At last spring came, the weather got warmer and the ice on the lake melted. The ugly duckling felt the sun on his feathers. "I think I'll go for a swim," he thought. He swam right out into the middle of the lake, where the water was as clear as a mirror. He looked down at his reflection in the water and stared and stared. Staring back at him was a beautiful white bird with a long, elegant neck. "I'm no longer an ugly duckling," he said to himself, "but what am I?"

At that moment three big white birds just like himself flew towards him and landed on the lake. They swam right up to him and one of them said, "You are the handsomest swan that we have ever seen. Would you care to join us?"

"So *that's* what I am – I'm a swan," thought the bird that had been an ugly duckling. "I would love to join you," he said to the other swans. "Am I really a swan?" he asked, not quite believing it could be true.

"Of course you are!" replied the others. "Can't you see you're just like us?"

The three older swans became his best friends and the ugly duckling, that was now a beautiful swan, swam across the lake with them and there they lived together. He knew that he was one of them and that he would never be lonely again.

Puss in Boots

Once upon a time in France, there lived a miller who had three sons. When he died, the miller left the mill to his eldest son. To his second son he left a donkey on whose back sacks of flour could be loaded and delivered to customers. But to the youngest son, who was much the most handsome of the three, he left only a large cat, whose job it had been to chase the mice that came at night to make holes in the sacks and steal grain.

The poor youngest brother wondered how on earth he would make his living with only the cat for company. He could see that he would have to go out into the world to seek his fortune. "I shall have to leave you behind, Puss," he said, "for I don't see how I am to look after you."

"What about if I looked after *you*?" replied Puss.

"Whatever do you mean?" said his master.

"I can make your fortune for you," said the cat. "All I need is a good – sized drawstring bag and a pair of really nice boots – for my hind feet."

Well, the lad was mightily puzzled, but he decided it was worth letting the cat try to win his fortune, as he surely had no idea of what to do otherwise. With his brand new boots on his hind paws and his drawstring bag slung over his shoulder, Puss set off with nothing but a handful of corn from the mill.

The first thing he did was go straight to the nearest rabbit warren where he opened the bag, put a little corn into it and laid it open near the rabbit hole. Then Puss laid in wait until dusk, when the rabbits came out of their hole. One rabbit came up, full of curiosity, and hopped into the bag to get the corn. Up sprang Puss and pulled the drawstring tight. Then, instead of taking the rabbit to his master, he set off to the palace, where he announced that he had brought the king a present.

"Your majesty," said Puss, taking a low bow, "I am a messenger from the Marquis of Carabas, your neighbour. He was out hunting today and was lucky enough to catch a fine young rabbit. He begs that you will accept it as a present."

The king was puzzled, because he'd never heard of this Marquis, but he was pleased to have the rabbit. "Tell your master that I am delighted with his kind present," he said.

Day after day, Puss went out hunting in this manner and each time he presented his catch to the king. "Don't forget," he said to his master, "that you're supposed to be a Marquis." The young boy had no idea what the cat was talking about, but he trusted him nevertheless. After a while the cat started to be invited in for a drink and a chat with the guards and he soon got to know all the court gossip. One time, Puss got to hear that the king was planning to drive the next day in his grand carriage with his daughter, the most beautiful princess in France. Puss took care to find out which direction they intended to take.

The next morning he said to his master, "I think it would be a good idea to take a swim in the river this morning." The lad agreed and, by the look in Puss's eye, he knew that he had a plan in mind. Puss led the way to a part of the river where the royal carriage was bound to pass. While the boy was swimming in the river, Puss heard the sound of the approaching carriage. Quickly Puss hid his master's ragged clothes under a stone and as the carriage came into view he ran into the road shouting, "Help! The Marquis of Carabas is drowning!" At once the king recognised Puss and ordered his guards to go to the rescue. The lad pretended to be drowning, so that the guards had quite a struggle to get him to the bank.

Meanwhile, Puss went up to the carriage, bowed to the king and said, "While he was bathing, thieves unfortunately stole my master's fine clothing. He cannot appear before your daughter without any clothes."

"Of course not," replied the king, and sent his footman to fetch a spare set of clothes from the back of the royal carriage. Now that the handsome lad was properly dressed, the king was glad to meet the mysterious Marquis, of whom he had heard so much from Puss. He welcomed the 'Marquis' into the carriage, where he sat next to the princess. "Come for a drive with us, my dear Marquis," said the king.

Without another word Puss set off and disappeared around the next bend of the road. By the time the king's gilded carriage was on its way again, Puss was a long way ahead. Soon he passed a field of haymakers. "My good haymakers," said Puss, "you must tell the king that this meadow belongs to the Marquis of Carabas – or I'll grind you all to little pieces."

Now Puss knew that the meadow really belonged to an ogre, who was known to be able to change his shape. So of course the haymakers had no idea if this was just an ordinary pussy cat telling them what to do – or if it really was the ogre. Soon the royal carriage passed by and the king leaned out and asked to whom the field belonged. "To the Marquis of Carabas, your majesty," chorused the haymakers.

"That's a fine piece of land you've got there," said the king, nudging the lad who was busy chatting to the princess.

All along the road it was the same story. Puss always got there before the royal carriage. Woodcutters, shepherds, and farmers all told the king that their master was the Marquis of Carabas, because Puss had threatened to turn them all into mincemeat if they didn't. Now Puss caught sight of a fine castle which he recognised as belonging to the ogre.

Puss went up to the great gate and asked to speak to the ogre. Puss said to him, "I heard that you can transform yourself in the most amazing way – into a lion for example. But I really can't believe that this is true."

The ogre was so offended that he bellowed, "JUST YOU WATCH!" and instantly turned himself into a lion. Puss pretended to be scared and jumped up on to the castle roof. The ogre turned himself back into an ogre. "That'll teach you," he roared.

"You gave me a dreadful fright," said Puss. "Do you know, people say you can even turn yourself into a tiny animal, such as rat or mouse. But that's absurd. It's quite impossible."

"IMPOSSIBLE, EH?" screeched the ogre, and the great foolish creature turned himself into a mouse.

In an instant, Puss had pounced on him and gobbled him up, bones and all. At that moment, the royal carriage rumbled over the drawbridge, for the king, too, had spotted the castle and wondered who lived there.

"Welcome to the castle of the Marquis of Carabas, your majesty," said Puss, who had just wiped the last morsels of the ogre from his whiskers.

"What," cried the king, turning to the young boy, "is this yours, too?"   The lad glanced at Puss and then nodded. "May we see inside?" went on the king.

So the king, the princess and the miller's son looked around the castle. And very fine it was, too. The ogre's servants were so happy to see the back of their master that they laid on a fine feast. And at the end of the meal, the king agreed to give his daughter's hand in marriage to the 'Marquis'.

As for Puss, his master was so grateful that he saw to it that the cat was made a lord. So they all lived happily ever after and Puss never had to chase another mouse for the rest of his life.

The Wolf and the Seven Goats

There was once an old mother goat who had seven little goats.
They all lived in a tiny house on the edge of a big, dark forest.
One day, the mother goat had to go into the forest to collect food.
Before she left, she called her seven little goats to her and said,
"Now, children, promise me that while I am away you will lock
the door and be on your guard against the wicked wolf. If you see
him, don't let him in, because he would certainly eat you all up.
You can recognize him by his gruff voice and his big black paws."

"Yes, mother," the little goats replied, "we promise to be very
careful."

So the mother goat trotted cheerfully away into the forest, and the little goats locked the door. Some time later, there was a knock at the door, and the little goats heard a voice calling, "Open the door, children, it is your mother. I have brought back a present for each of you."

But the little goats heard that the voice was gruff, and not the gentle voice of their mother, and so they called, "No, we will not let you in! You do not have a soft voice like our mother's, you have a gruff voice. You are the wolf!"

So the cunning wolf went to a shop and stole a jar of syrup and swallowed it to make his voice soft. Then back he went to the little house by the forest. "Open the door, children," he called in his new, soft voice. "It is your mother. I have brought back a present for each of you."

Now the little goats heard the soft voice, but in his eagerness to get into the house the wolf had put his big black paws on to the window ledge, and so the little goats cried out, "No, we will not let you in! Our mother has beautiful white feet, but you have black feet. You are the wolf!"

So the wolf ran back into the village and went to the baker's shop, where he stole some flour and covered his paws in it. The wolf ran back to the little house by the forest. "Children, children, open the door!" he called again. "It is your mother. I have brought back a present for each of you."

The little goats heard the soft voice but they could not see any paws, and they called out, "Let us see your paws so that we know you really are our mother." So the wolf lifted up his paws, which of course were all white from the flour plastered on them. The little goats thought that this time it really was their mother, and they unlocked the door.

The wolf rushed in. The little goats screamed and tried to hide. One jumped into a drawer; the second squeezed under the bed; the third buried itself in the bedclothes; the fourth leaped into a cupboard; the fifth went into the oven; the sixth hid under a basin; and the littlest one slipped inside the grandfather clock. But the wolf found them and gobbled them up – all except the youngest one hiding in the grandfather clock. When the wolf had finished his meal, he felt very full and very sleepy. He wandered out of the house into a nearby meadow, lay down on some dry leaves, and promptly fell asleep.

When the mother goat came home from the forest, imagine her horror as she saw the door open, the furniture strewn around the house and the little goats all gone. She started calling them by name, but nobody answered until she called out the name of the youngest little goat, who was still hiding in the grandfather clock. She quickly pulled him out, and then he told her what had happened to all his brothers and sisters.

She ran out of the house with the little goat trotting beside her and soon found the wolf sleeping in the meadow. She looked carefully at him and saw that there were six lumps in his fat stomach, and that they seemed to be moving. "My little goats are still alive," she exclaimed with joy.

Quickly she sent the youngest goat back to her house for scissors, needle and thread. Then, while the wolf was still sleeping, she carefully cut a hole in the wolf's stomach. Soon a little goat popped out and then another and another, until all six were free and jumping for joy. They had not come to any harm, for in his greed the wolf had swallowed them all whole.

"Quick," cried the mother goat, "fetch me some rocks from the river so that I can fill up this wicked wolf's stomach." So the little goats each fetched a rock and the mother goat sewed them up inside the wolf's stomach.

When the wolf awoke, he was very thirsty. "What is the matter with me?" he thought. "I shouldn't have eaten all those goats at once. Now I've got indigestion." He set out to drink from the river. But his stomach was so heavy he could hardly walk and he staggered to the water's edge. As he bent over to drink, the weight of the stones pulled the wolf into the water, where he sank straight to the bottom and drowned. Then the mother goat and all her little goats – who had been watching – danced for joy. For never again would they be afraid of the wicked wolf!

Rapunzel

There once lived a man and his wife who had long wished for a child. At last their wish was granted and the wife found that she was expecting a baby. At the back of their house was a garden that was filled with the most beautiful flowers and herbs. However, the man and his wife did not dare enter the garden, for it was owned by a wicked witch, of whom everyone was scared.

One day, when the woman was standing by her window looking down into the garden, she saw a flower bed full of the prettiest Rapunzel plants she had ever seen. They looked so fresh and green that she felt a great craving to eat some of them. Day after day she would sit by her window, staring at the Rapunzel plants for hours on end. Eventually she became quite pale and miserable.

88

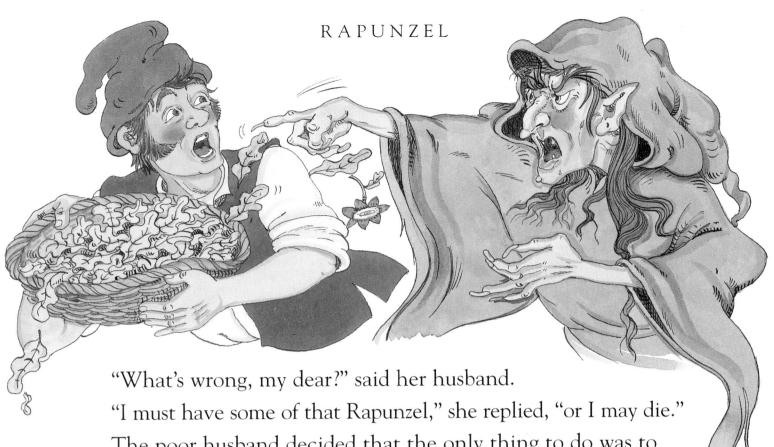

"What's wrong, my dear?" said her husband.

"I must have some of that Rapunzel," she replied, "or I may die."

The poor husband decided that the only thing to do was to steal into the witch's garden at night and take some of the plants. Late one night the man climbed the high wall that surrounded the garden and hastily snatched a bunch of Rapunzel plants and made off with them.

His wife was delighted. She made a salad of them that was so delicious that the next day she said to her husband, "I must have more of that delicious Rapunzel."

So that night the husband stole once more into the witch's garden. Imagine his horror when he dropped on to the grass to find the witch there lying in wait for him. "How dare you come into my garden and steal my Rapunzel plants," she shrieked. "You'll live to regret this."

"Please have mercy on me," begged the man. "I'm not really a thief. I came to help my wife, who is expecting our first child. She told me she would die if she didn't have some of your Rapunzel to eat."

Then the witch changed her tune. "By all means," she said, "take as much as you like. But in exchange you must give me the baby when it is born. Don't worry – I will care for it as if I were its mother. What do you say?" The man was so terrified that he hastily agreed to what the witch had said. When his wife gave birth to a baby girl the witch immediately appeared to take the child. The witch named her Rapunzel, after the plants that had caused all the trouble, and took the child away with her.

Rapunzel grew very beautiful, strong and healthy, with long golden hair that fell past her waist. When she was twelve years old the witch locked her away at the top of a tower in the middle of a forest. The tower had neither stairs nor a door, but only one window at the top so that nobody but the witch could reach her.

Each day when the witch visited her, she would stand below the girl's window and call out, "Rapunzel, Rapunzel, let down your hair, that I may climb without a stair."

Then the girl would wind her long tresses around the window hook and lower her hair all the way to the ground. The witch would climb up it as if it were a ladder. In this way, Rapunzel's lonely life went on for several years.

One day, a young prince was riding in the forest when he heard a sweet voice. It was Rapunzel singing to herself. The prince was so entranced that he followed the sound and came upon the tower.

But when he could find no way in he became discouraged
and rode home. Rapunzel's lovely voice had stirred his heart so
deeply, however, that he returned day after day to hear her
singing.

One day, as he stood behind a tree, he saw the witch appear
and heard her calling, "Rapunzel, Rapunzel, let down your hair,
that I may climb without a stair."

Then he saw a mass of golden hair tumble down and watched
the witch climb up it to the window. "Is that the way up?"
thought the prince. "Then I will climb the golden ladder, too."

The next day, around dusk, the prince went to the tower and
called, "Rapunzel, Rapunzel, let down your hair, that I may climb
without a stair."

Immediately the tresses fell down and the prince climbed up. At first sight of the prince, Rapunzel was afraid, but the prince addressed her in such a friendly way that she knew she could trust him. "Once I had heard your voice," said the prince, "I couldn't rest until I saw you. Now I cannot rest until you agree to marry me."

Rapunzel by now had fallen truly in love with the young man, so she willingly accepted. "I wish I could come away with you," said Rapunzel. "You must bring some silk with you each time you visit, and I shall weave a ladder of silk and then I will be able to escape."

Each day the witch visited Rapunzel and each night the prince came. The witch suspected nothing until one day Rapunzel forgot herself and said to the witch, "Why are you so much heavier to pull up than the prince?"

"Oh, treacherous girl," screamed the witch. "You have deceived me!" She snatched up a pair of scissors and cut off all Rapunzel's lovely hair. Then the witch drove Rapunzel from the tower and left her in a wild and desolate place to fend for herself as best she could.

That night, along came the prince to the tower and said, as usual, "Rapunzel, Rapunzel, let down your hair, that I may climb without a stair."

But the witch was lying in wait. She tied Rapunzel's hair to the window hook and let the golden tresses fall to the ground. Up climbed the prince full of joy, as always. But when he stepped in through the window, it was not his beautiful Rapunzel that met his gaze but the icy glare of the witch. "Aha!" cried the witch with a sneer. "So you thought you could steal my girl, did you? Well she's gone and you'll never set eyes on her again."

Beside himself with grief, the prince threw himself from the tower and would have died had he not landed in the thickest briars. Although he survived, the thorns pierced his eyes and blinded him. For many years he wandered through the wilderness grieving for his lost Rapunzel and living on whatever he could find to eat. Eventually, he wandered into the same part of the wilderness where Rapunzel lived in miserable poverty with the twins she had borne.

Just as he had done so many years ago, the prince heard a sweet voice coming through the trees. He made his way towards the sound of the voice. Suddenly Rapunzel saw him and straight away she recognised him. She ran to him and threw her arms around him weeping. As she wept tears of joy and sorrow, two teardrops fell into his eyes, healing them and restoring his sight.

Then the two were united again and the prince took Rapunzel and their children back to his own kingdom, and they all lived happily ever after.